GW00370744

SOWLN

Please return/renew this item by the last date shown on this label, or on your self-service receipt.

To renew this item, visit **www.librarieswest.org.uk** or contact your library

Your borrower number and PIN are required.

1 3 1812713 6

Catie Zorn

The Kitchen Cupboard Fairies

© 2022 **Europe Books**| London
www.europebooks.co.uk | info@europebooks.co.uk

ISBN 9791220127066
First edition: October 2022

Illustrations by Maria Cassoni

The Kitchen Cupboard Fairies

*I dedicate this book to my Mother and Father.
My Mum told me many enchanting stories
when I was young.
My Father's love of literature
has been my inspiration.*

Table of Contents

Chapter One
The Fairies

All the children loved Zelda. She was always happy and welcomed them on her "Cooking with Kids" programme each day, with a big smile and a warm hug. With Zelda they made cookies, cakes and healthy snacks for their own lunchboxes and proudly took them home.

Zelda loved the children and she loved cooking. In fact, she loved cooking so much that she spent her time at home in her own kitchen, being busy creating delicious meals for her family and friends.

Her kitchen was big, bright and full of the most amazing gadgets and cooking tools. The white granite worktops contrasted with the grey and black cupboards and the stainless steel appliances sitting on them, gleamed in the sunlight that streamed through the windows.

Zelda told everyone that she felt something magical happened when she created meals in her kitchen. She was right: there was something magical about her kitchen but she actually had no idea about it!

Zelda was not the only one who loved her kitchen, the fairies loved it too!

A family of fairies had been living comfortably in her kitchen cupboards for a few years now. When they had discovered the warm comfort of her kitchen they were thrilled. They had been homeless, searching for a new place to live for weeks. It had been so long that they had forgotten their names and where they had come from. Now they were living happily in the cupboard to the left of the dishwasher, which kept them warm and snug as it chugged away[1] washing the dirty dishes.

There were five of them, tiny pretty people not much taller than your littlest finger.

Cinnamon, the eldest and the head of the family, had a crop of brownish red hair and a pair of fairy-sized round spectacles, which rested on the end of his tiny nose. The spectacles had been given to him by his great-grandfather when he had learnt to read.

It was by reading the labels on the packets and jars in the cupboards of Zelda's kitchen that Cinnamon had helped the fairies choose their new names, just after they had set up home in the kitchen cupboard.

Vanilla, Cinnamon's wife, helped him to keep the other fairies in order. Although she was quite old now, she was still very beautiful. She kept her very long white hair piled up on top of her head with the help of one of Zelda's freezer ties and several cocktail sticks. Around her neck and tiny wrists were circles of creamy white pearls.

---

[1] To continue working

Coriander, Tarragon and Tabasco were the young fairies. They were mostly well behaved but often needed the guidance of Cinnamon and Vanilla.

The fairies had made themselves very comfortable in their cupboard. Shortly after they had found Zelda's kitchen, it was obvious that the cupboard to the left of the dishwasher would be a quiet warm safe place for them to live.

Zelda kept several wooden bowls in this cupboard; she really never used them anymore as she had far nicer trendy ones, but her mother had given them to her and she would have never thrown them out.

The wood was warm and the fairies cushioned[2] the bottom of the large bowl with kitchen paper and it made the perfect sleeping place for them. It was lovely snuggled in there together during the day, while the humming dishwasher kept the cupboard warm and Zelda bustled[3] about singing to herself as she cooked, creating delicious smells.

Often she would put on the television and watch her own cooking show. The fairies especially liked when Zelda did this because they could snooze and listen to the chatter of the children and imagine the things they were cooking.

It was in the daytime that the fairies slept, of course, because at night they had their adventures!

---

[2] To soften an impact
[3] Busy with something

Chapter Two
The Roundabout

Tabasco was an impatient fairy. He liked everything done straight away, he just could not wait. He also loved to be right and usually thought that he was and that he knew best about everything. His bright red hair and sharp turned up nose suited his impatient "know it all" ways, which often led to arguments with the other fairies, especially with Cinnamon.

Cinnamon had lived a long time; even he did not know quite how long and he was content to take his time over things.[4] He thought before he rushed into anything. Of course, because of his age and experience, he knew a lot about a lot of things. So sometimes Tabasco and Cinnamon found living together rather difficult.

"I really do get so tired of the arguing between you two." sighed Vanilla one night.

"Cinnamon, can you not just let Tabasco find out for himself how things should be done?"

"I would gladly leave him to his own devices if only I wasn't so worried about him getting into trouble and maybe leading Coriander and Tarragon into trouble with him." said Cinnamon.

"But then I expect one day he will learn, I just hope it's the easy way."

The latest argument was about the new revolving cake board which had appeared on the kitchen worktop the day before.

---

[4] To have the control over something

Zelda had promised to make a birthday cake for her niece's 6th birthday: it was a beautiful board made of shiny marble and she had left it out to admire it, as she was cooking dinner earlier that evening.

The young fairies loved the look of the cake board too. They suggested to Cinnamon that they should all investigate it together when they were sure Zelda and her husband had gone upstairs to bed. Cinnamon was interested, of course, but had said *soon* in a vague kind of way. This did not suit Tabasco! So he immediately started nagging[5] Cinnamon and an argument started.

Now Tabasco had gone off in a huff[6] to find Coriander and Tarragon, determined to go ahead regardless of Cinnamon, to investigate this new excitement right away.

Not surprisingly, Coriander and Tarragon were ready enough to follow Tabasco as he skipped lightly across the worktop towards the shiny bright surface of the cake board. It looked huge to the three young fairies as they stood on tiptoes looking at the top of it, just like a huge field would look to you.

Zelda had left a few of the things she would need to decorate the cake just beside the board: a packet of

---

[5] To complain, to be critical
[6] To leave in an angry manner

fondant icing, several small bottles of food colouring and an icing set.

"This will make decorating the cake so much easier, I can just move it around to put the rosebuds around the edge, so easy!" she had said to herself earlier.

The fairies used the packet of fondant icing to climb up onto the board. Tabasco was first, of course. As he stood there, he was a little bit daunted by the size of the *circular playground* but was determined to have fun, so he called to the other two:

"Come on up you two! It's super big! We will be able to run around forever up here!"

Coriander jumped up daintily[7] beside him.

"I'm glad I didn't crease my dress too much climbing up." she said smoothing the material of her pretty skirt.

Tarragon pulled himself up a little clumsily for a fairy and, as he landed on the surface of the board, something they had not expected happened. The whole *playground* moved!

"Oh"

"What's happening?"

"Did I do that?"

They all cried out at once and grabbed each other's hands.

When they had recovered a little bit, Tabasco lay down on his tummy and looked over the edge of the board. He could see a sort of disc underneath, which he guessed made the whole board go around. He stood up with a wide grin on his cheeky face.

"We are going to have some fun tonight!" he sang out to the other two.

---

[7] Delicately

Soon they realized that the board could be pushed by one of them quite easily if they stood on the worktop, and the other two could have a ride. It was indeed great fun! Even Coriander did not complain when her hair streamed out behind her as she sat, having her turn with Tabasco while Tarragon pushed them.

"Push a bit faster, Tarragon." shouted Tabasco.

"I can't, it's too heavy." puffed Tarragon.

"I know, let's have two of us pushing and one riding on, then we can each have a really fast ride." suggested Tabasco excitedly.

"Oh no, I don't want to go really fast!" squealed Coriander.

"Well, I do!" insisted Tabasco.

"You get off and push with Tarragon, Coriander, go on!"

Coriander had her doubts about this idea, but she knew it was no good arguing with Tabasco when he was so fired up about something, so off she got. It took a few minutes before the two fairies working together got up much speed pushing the board around, but soon it was spinning round so fast that they had to run to keep it going, as it seemed to gather more speed the more it turned around.

Squeals of delight came from the daredevil Tabasco, as he sat in the middle of the board with his head thrown back.

"Faster, faster!" he commanded.

And as the board spun faster, the silly fairy stood up and started doing tricks!

Tabasco stood on one leg then on the other, he hopped about unsteadily laughing and squealing as he teetered about and he stood on his hands. Then the trouble started!

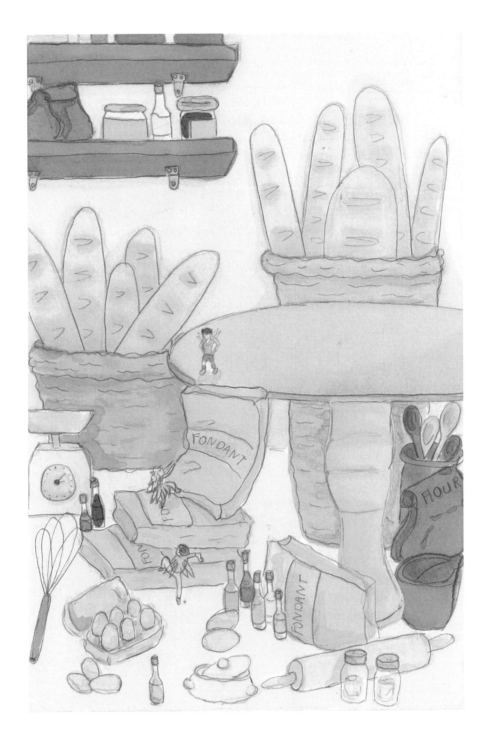

The speed of the board was too much and he was too light to stay in one place. Suddenly, as he embarked on a cartwheel stunt, he took off like a tiny bird and flew through the air! As he flew across the board and downwards, his squeals were no longer excited but scared.

Tabasco landed with a crash amongst the bottles of food colouring on the worktop. As he fell into them, the top came off the bright orange colour as it toppled over and Tabasco was covered from head to toe in sticky orange colouring. He sat there stunned for a few minutes.

Cinnamon and Vanilla, who had heard the crash, came running over whilst Coriander and Tarragon, feeling responsible for the accident, scuttled away to the corner.

Vanilla fussed over[8] Tabasco.

"Are you alright, my little one?" she asked, but not getting too close in case the bright orange colouring rubbed off on her.

Cinnamon stood with his arms folded across his tiny chest. He looked very annoyed shaking his head as he surveyed the scene in front of him.

---

[8] Be overly attentive

Seeing him, Tabasco stood up proudly, if a little shakily, and announced:

"Of course I am alright, it was the best fun ever and this colour matches my hair beautifully!"

It obviously did not suit him though to be covered in the sticky liquid, for he spent the rest of the night under the kitchen tap trying to wash off the ghastly[9] orange stuff from his skin and clothes.

"Do you think that is the easy way to learn, Cinnamon?" whispered Vanilla as they all settled down to sleep just before dawn.

"Do you think he has learned from the experience, Vanilla?" replied Cinnamon.

---

[9] Terrifying

Later when the others were fast asleep and she was sure that Zelda was out, Vanilla retrieved her shiny silver wand from beneath her other precious treasures in her special box, and she crept up[10] onto the worktop.

A quick spell and a touch of her wand, and the mess from last night's accident disappeared in a flash of silver light. Then, Vanilla crept quietly back to the warm safety of their wooden bowl.

Later on in the day, when the fairies were beginning to wake up, but knew they had to stay quiet until night time, they heard the title music of "Cooking With Zelda".

Zelda was making dinner and watching her latest show. The fairies listened to Zelda explaining to the children that they were about to make oat cookies.

The children talked and laughed with Zelda as they weighed out the ingredients. At the thought of those delicious cookies their tiny fairy tummies began to rumble!

---

[10] Approach in a furtive way

Chapter Three
Spaghetti

Zelda was very tired after a long day at the TV studio. They had been working on the new series of programmes and the beginning stage was always hard. She was filmed making the recipes that she would use with the children on the show; it was hard work and not much fun without the children.

With a big sigh she put her bags down on the table and decided a quick meal was in order. She was very hungry but really she had had enough of cooking for one day, however much she loved it!

So what to have?

"Ahh yes" she thought to herself "spaghetti with some pesto sauce from the freezer."

Zelda was very organised in her kitchen and she made her own sauces and froze them into individual pots, ready for just this sort of occasion.

She filled a large saucepan with water, put it on the hob and lit the gas, added just a drizzle of olive oil to stop the spaghetti from sticking together, got out the sauce and popped it into the microwave to defrost. Easy!

Just a short time later, she was straining the spaghetti into a colander in the sink when her mobile rang out with the tones of "Food Glorious Food".

Zelda sighed a little impatiently and answered with a cheery "Hello" as she could manage.

It was the producer of her show and not good news.

"Hello Zelda, sorry to do this but we need you to come back and film the last section again"

"Oh dear, the last section, why?" asked Zelda.

"Yes, the chocolate brownies, we did not get a very good shot of you taking them out of the oven. You are supposed to turn to the children and show them how yummy they look and smile. Perhaps you were a bit tired, and, I am sorry, but we do need to wrap this up today. Can you be here in half an hour?"

Zelda looked longingly at her dinner but said "Of course, I'll be there. No problem!"

" You are great, Zelda. See you soon."

Zelda sighed again but quickly lifted the colander out of the sink and put it on the kitchen counter for when she got back.

The brownie filming took a bit longer than expected and afterwards the producer, very sportingly, took Zelda and the rest of the team out for dinner.

So when Zelda got home again, the spaghetti was left where she had put it because she was then not simply tired, but absolutely exhausted and she went straight to bed falling asleep in seconds!

As darkness fell, the fairies woke and one by one they came out of their cupboard to the left of the dishwasher ready for the night's adventures.

Coriander had slept particularly well and she was in a very happy mood.

"Come on you two" she called to Tarragon and Tabasco,

"The three of us should play together tonight and have some fun!" the boys exchanged amused glances.

This was a pretty rare occurrence, but they knew they would enjoy, as when Coriander was in a good mood she really was so much fun!

They eagerly scrambled up onto the kitchen counter after her. The three of them skipped along holding hands and Coriander sang sweetly as they went across the huge

23

surface. She circled around them, ducking under their arms and pulling them under after her until they were all laughing and quite dizzy.

They came to a halt[11] tumbling over each other, enjoying the space and stretching their legs after their long sleep in their warm salad bowl.

"I could climb a mountain I feel so full of energy" said Tarragon.

"I could fly to the moon...and back, and that is much more difficult" said Tabasco competitively.

"Now, now you two don't start" scolded Coriander.

"If you argue it will be no fun at all."

But Tarragon wasn't paying attention to either of them. He had seen something very interesting and unusual.

---

[11] To stop suddenly

It was huge and silver and had a lot of holes in it, with long strings of something pale yellow poking out of some of the holes. He had no idea what it could possibly be, but there was no doubt in his mind that it had to be investigated!

"Hey, you two, come and look at this amazing *thing* with me" he called them.

Coriander and Tabasco hurried after Tarragon and soon saw the *thing* he was referring to.

Coriander came to an abrupt halt and stood, looking both scared and intrigued.

"What on earth is that?" she said.

Tabasco was just standing there looking from the *thing* to Tarragon. Their eyes met and they both grinned. As both the boys ran forwards, Coriander summoned up her courage and followed them.

At first, they slowly circled what was, of course, the colander full of spaghetti that Zelda had hurriedly left on the kitchen counter when she had to rush back to the studio.

There were strands of spaghetti hanging out of the holes of the colander and Tabasco, being the most impetuous of the three fairies, was the first to pull on one strand. It was quite easy to pull it through the hole, it was still slippery with the olive oil that Zelda had added to the water to stop it from sticking.

All three of the fairies were wide-eyed with wonder, as the long string of this amazing stuff continued to come through the hole. It was so long!

Tabasco had to keep walking backwards as he pulled and it got longer and longer. He was almost at the edge of the kitchen counter, when the end finally dropped out of the hole onto the counter.

They stood for just a few seconds looking at it, and when it seemed clear that it was not going to harm them, they all started pulling on more of the strands that were sticking through the holes.

All three of them were giggling[12] and cheering as each string of spaghetti in turn came free of the colander. When each of them had pulled three springs free, they stood looking at them spread across the kitchen counter.

Tarragon looked a bit disappointed, he had thought this strange *thing* might be something more interesting. But now all they had was a pile of sticky strands.

"Well, that is the end of that" he said

"Yes, not really much fun now, is it?" commented Tabasco.

Coriander smiled slowly and then she jumped up and down, clapping her tiny hands and shouted "SKIPPING!"

The boys looked a bit puzzled but Coriander picked up the end of one of the long strings and held it out for Tabasco to take from her, then she ran lightly to the other end and held that out for Tarragon to take from her.

"Now!" she said bossily

"You two turn this stringy thing over and over so that it loops and I will try skipping."

Not at all sure what *skipping* was, they dutifully tried to turn the string. It was hard at first as they were turning it in different directions, but eventually they got the hang of it.

Coriander tucked in her wings and counted "1, 2, 3" then she gracefully stepped forward and jumped at just the right time, so the string went neatly under her tiny

---

[12] To laugh

feet. Then, as it was above her head, she jumped again and, just as before, the string passed easily under her feet.

"I'm skipping!" she sang out happily.

Both Tarragon and Tabasco were impressed and watched her entranced, as they continued to turn the string of spaghetti for her.

"I want to try now!" shouted Tabasco.

"Me too!" shouted Tarragon.

Coriander could have carried on all night; she was so enjoying skipping. She had read about it in one of the magazines which Vanilla looked at sometimes. But she was a kind and generous fairy and knew that she should share this with the others. She stopped and walked over, taking the end of the string of spaghetti from Tabasco.

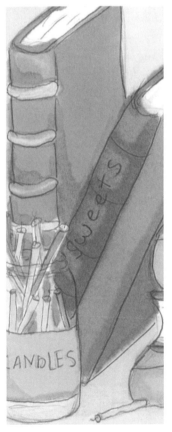

Tabasco stood watching Coriander and Tarragon turned the string over and over, as he was determined to get this right.

He stepped forward and jumped! But, oh dear, he miss-timed it, stood on the spaghetti and it broke! He was annoyed, it had looked so easy when Coriander did it, why could he not do it?

"No matter" said Coriander quickly, as she ran to get another string and passed one end to Tarragon.

"Just try again, you will soon get the hang of it"

"No!" said Tabasco irritably

"You try, Tarragon"

He was secretly hoping that Tarragon would not be able to skip then he would not feel so silly.

Tarragon took a deep breath and jumped, just as the string came down, and he did it! Then he jumped again, and once again the string passed under his feet. He was grinning widely and enjoying himself very much. But he stopped and asked Tabasco:

"Would you like another try, Tabasco? It's easier than you think!"

"No, I think there must be more interesting things to do with this stuff" he said huffily[13].

He began tying a loose knot in the end he was holding, and made a lasso loop.

Coriander was not the only one who looked at Vanilla's magazines, he had seen a picture of a man on horseback holding something like this. He whirled it above his head a couple of times then threw it towards the pepper mill on the kitchen counter. It looped neatly over the top and, as Tabasco pulled it, toppled over!

"Yes!" he shouted triumphantly

"I can do something even better than skipping!"

"Wow, that is good" said Tarragon admiringly.

Now Coriander and Tarragon both copied Tabasco and made loose knots in the ends of the strings of spaghetti, trying to lasso the spice jars standing along the back of kitchen counter.

They were not as successful as Tabasco, and although they tried again and again, they just could not do it.

---

[13] Arrogantly

Tabasco was busy throwing his lasso over all different things and having a great time. He was feeling happy after having shown he could do something the other two could not do.

As Coriander and Tarragon tried yet again, they managed to get their lassos caught up mid-air and they came down together, knocking several of the spice jars over with a huge crash!

All three fairies stood very still. They knew that they should always be careful to be as quiet as possible in case they woke Zelda up. Holding their breath they waited. Fortunately, Zelda was not disturbed; so tired was she that she was sleeping very soundly.

But Cinnamon and Vanilla had certainly heard the noise, and they came hurrying across to the young fairies.

"What is happening here?" demanded Cinnamon crossly.

"You cannot make all this noise, you know better than this."

"Oh, dear me!" cried Vanilla "Are you all alright, are you hurt in any way?"

They assured her they were fine.

"We found this stuff, Cinnamon, and we were just having some fun with it. We really did not mean to make a noise or this mess." said Coriander.

She turned to the boys:

"We are so sorry, aren't we?"

Both the boy fairies nodded and muttered[14] their apologies too.

"Well" said Cinnamon.

"You had better wash the stickiness off your hands and go to bed, it's nearly getting light anyway. Vanilla and I will take care of the mess you have made."

They said thank you and goodnight and walked slowly towards their cupboard.

"Right" said Vanilla.

"I will sort this out, Cinnamon, no need for you to worry."

She took out her wand, and with a couple of showers of glitter and some magic words, all was as it should be once more.

As she walked back to their cupboard, Cinnamon said:

"Thank you, Vanilla, you are always so calm and efficient in a crisis. I just worry that one night those three

---

[14] To murmur

will do something and then we will be discovered and have to move again."

Vanilla patted his arm and said:

"You know, Cinnamon, I sometimes think that if Zelda did know about us she would be very happy to have us here."

Cinnamon hoped she was right. She usually was, but that night she had been just a bit too efficient and she had actually magically cleared up all the mess, every last string of spaghetti had disappeared!

The next morning, when Zelda came into the kitchen to make her coffee, she looked at the empty colander with a puzzled frown.

"I was sure I didn't throw the spaghetti out" he said to herself "perhaps in my rush to get back to the studio I did."

But when she checked the bin and there was no spaghetti she was still very puzzled.

"Funny things happen in my kitchen" she laughed to herself "I'm glad I am not so absent minded in the studio kitchen!"

Chapter Four
A Bed fit for a Princess

Coriander was a very pretty fairy. Now you probably think that all fairies are pretty and you are probably right! But Coriander was the prettiest fairy you could imagine.

She had beautiful long silver blonde hair, which fell in shimmering ringlets down her back all the way to just below her waist, and wispy curls framed her tiny face.

She had large sapphire blue eyes, a pretty little nose and a perfect pink mouth which broke easily into the most enchanting smile.

Coriander was lovely and she adored lovely things. Her clothes were made of the finest and most delicate fairy silks. Her favourite dress was a pale powder blue with silver threads, which matched perfectly with her silver wings.

One night, Coriander was walking on her own around the kitchen shelves where Zelda kept her cookery books. Tarragon and Tabasco had asked her to play with them, but that night, dressed in her favourite dress, she did not feel like the rough-and-tumble[15] of one of the boys games.

She often walked with Vanilla, she loved talking with her and hearing the stories of when Vanilla was a young fairy and almost as beautiful as Coriander herself. But that night Vanilla was busy measuring Cinnamon for a new suit of clothes. So Coriander was strolling contentedly around[16] on her own, humming to herself.

---

[15] Rude
[16] Take a walk

It was especially nice walking along the cookery book shelf, there were so many lovely pictures to look at on the covers of the books.

As she walked along, she came across a new thing she had never seen before! The "new thing" was an empty matchbox, which Zelda had left on the shelf after lighting the candles on the birthday cake yesterday.

Coriander skipped daintily over to investigate. She walked around the box once. Then, being a cautious little fairy, she walked around it another three times. Now she was satisfied that it looked safe enough to touch. She pushed gently on one end of it, the inside moved a bit!

She skipped round to the other end and saw that the sort of drawer part was open a little way.

Coriander gasped excitedly and peeped inside[17], expecting it to be full of wonderful treasures, but When she saw that it was empty she was disappointed.

Coriander had an imaginative mind, and at once she began to wonder what she could make of this new and interesting discovery.

Then it struck her[18] that it looked very much like a bed she had once seen in a picture book about a princess! She climbed into it and, yes, it was a perfect size for her. She imagined that with a few satin pillows and covers, it would really be very cosy and grand. She ran off to find the others to see if they would help her carry it back to their cupboard.

With everyone helping, the "bed" was soon taken to the cupboard to the left of the dishwasher where the fairies lived. But as try as they might, they could not lift it up and into their bowl.

---

[17] To look furtively
[18] To realize

It was just impossible because the box was bigger than they were, even bigger than Tabasco, and he was tall for a fairy.

Coriander looked so sad. She would not be able to sleep in her beautiful new bed after all, her pretty eyes filled with silvery tears. Then she had an idea! She could sleep in her bed where it was just beside the bowl. She was sure she was brave enough, in fact she would probably be feeling so special and grand that she would not feel the tiniest bit lonely or afraid. She breathlessly told the others her plan.

Vanilla was not at all happy about the proposed idea when Coriander excitedly suggested it.

"You may not be safe, dear" she said.

"I would much rather you sleep in with us all as usual. What do you think, Cinnamon?"

Surprisingly, Cinnamon did not seem to think there would be a problem.

"She will not come to any harm, Vanilla, and she can always call us if she needs us"

Secretly, he did not think that Coriander would be brave enough to stay alone, so he could see no point in arguing this matter with her. A wink at Vanilla and she understood him at once, smiling at Coriander.

"Alright, then let's find you some pretty things to make your new bed comfortable" she said.

Coriander spent the rest of the night making her bed into a bed fit for a princess.

Vanilla gave her some pieces of lovely soft satin in pink and lilac shades to use for her pillow and covers. She worked hard and she was delighted with the result.

Tabasco and Tarragon had found her some lacy ribbon and they helped her drape it over the top of the matchbox, so that the final finished bed looked perfect.

Tabasco was a bit put out that he was not allowed to "camp out" too, for it was just the sort of adventure he loved. But for once he was patient and happy that Coriander was getting such a treat.

As dawn was just breaking, Coriander stood back and surveyed her work.

"A bed fit for a princess" she sighed happily.

She already had butterflies in her tummy at the thought of sleeping away from the others, but she was determined to sleep at least one night as a princess.

When they were all ready for bed, they kissed Coriander and said "Good-night" before they climbed up to snuggle down together in their bowl.

"Sweet dreams" called Vanilla softly.

She knew neither herself nor Cinnamon would get any sleep as long as Coriander stayed outside in her bed, but she wondered how long that would be.

Coriander climbed carefully into her bed and slipped down between the silky sheets. They felt cool, soft and special. She lay there for a few minutes feeling excited and not a bit sleepy.

She closed her eyes, she tried counting snowflakes - a trick, Vanilla said, always helped fairies who found going to sleep difficult. She shuffled a bit. It was a very comfy bed but

she felt strange without the
others snuggled into her.

"I am going to sleep
here, though." she told
herself determinedly.

"I have always wanted a
bedroom of my own. I will
sing very softly to myself
until I fall asleep."

And that is what she did.
Her gentle voice was heard
by Vanilla and Cinnamon.

"At least we know she is
safe whilst we can hear her
singing, don't we?" said Vanilla.

"Yes" he yawned in reply and drifted into a light sleep,
always with one ear open should Coriander call.

Coriander sang to herself nearly all through the day.
Now and again she nodded off to sleep, but jerked awake
again quickly as she remembered where she was
sleeping. The sound of the television when Zelda turned
on her cooking show seemed much louder outside the
bowl, but Coriander was comforted by the children's
voices.

Vanilla did not sleep at all!

That evening all the fairies, except Tabasco and
Tarragon, were tired. As tired as she was, Coriander was
pleased with herself for being brave but very happy to get
up and have the others around her again. While she was
making her bed tidy, Vanilla came over to her:

"Your singing was lovely, Coriander, but I don't think
you slept very much, did you?"

Reluctantly, Coriander admitted that she had not slept
at all really.

Vanilla knew how she felt and gave her an opportunity to give in, without feeling she would not be brave enough to sleep on her own again.

"You know, Coriander, that box-bed would be the perfect place to keep all your special things, your pretty beads and sparkly jewels" she said.

Coriander smiled with relief and hugged Vanilla. She spent the rest of the day arranging her treasures in her box-bed. Then she snuggled down with the others as dawn was breaking and went to sleep immediately.

Chapter Five
Strawberry Gateau

Z elda stood back and surveyed her work. Yes, she was pleased, the strawberry gateau she had created for tomorrow's end of season party looked beautiful.

"The end of my fourth television series with the children" she said to herself.

"Who would have dreamed that my cooking would make me a star!"

This season of "Cooking with Zelda" had been the best yet. The four children she had spent the season cooking with had been such fun and she was sad it was over, but looking forward to the party the day after.

She carefully covered the gateau loosely with silver foil and tucked the edges under the plate.

"That will keep it safe" she said.

"Now I'm off to bed, I'm so tired" Zelda climbed the stairs to her bedroom yawning.

"I'm bored!" groaned Tarragon later that night.

"What can I do?"

"Well, you could tidy yourself up a bit for a start" said Vanilla.

"It must be ages since you've combed your hair and your wings are all dusty."

Tarragon did not care much about how he looked. *Smart* was not a word anyone would use to describe him! Even when he made an effort to look better he never quite got it right.

But his carefree and happy nature made up for his lack of smartness. Tarragon liked to please people too so he said:

"I'll try then, Vanilla. Perhaps you could help me with my wings, Coriander, they are difficult for me to reach."

"I don't think I want to get all dusty helping you to clean your wings,. Thank you, Tarragon. Why don't you ask Tabasco?" said Coriander primly.

"Now, Coriander, that is not very nice!" chided[19] Cinnamon, looking up from the tiny piece of newspaper he was reading.

"Help Tarragon to smarten himself up, there's a good girl, then you can all do something fun for the rest of the night."

Reluctantly, Coriander got up to help Tarragon. She worked hard brushing his wings carefully with a feather, they were very dusty indeed! Then she helped wipe down his suit with a tiny piece of dish cloth. Finally, she combed his hair for him using her own hairbrush which she had found in a dolls playset, which one of Zelda's nieces had left behind after visiting.

"I'll have to wash this later" she muttered to herself.

Everyone was impressed with Tarragon's appearance after Coriander had finished, and Tarragon strutted[20] up and down the worktop feeling very handsome, just like a fairy model!

"I'm really going to try to stay smart now" he announced to everyone.

He started to skip about, and Coriander and Tabasco joined in laughing together.

"Let's play something" suggested Tabasco.

"What about hide and seek? We haven't played that for ages!"

It was agreed. Tarragon and Coriander would hide first and Tabasco would count to 100, then try to find them both. The two fairies scampered off[21].

---

[19] To express disapproval
[20] To walk proudly
[21] To run quickly

"1, 2, 3, 4, 5…" started Tabasco.

Coriander looked around the shelves in the kitchen trying to see a nice place to hide. Eventually, she chose to climb carefully into the big fruit basket on the window sill. She loved the fresh smell of the oranges and apples, and she settled down patiently to wait until Tabasco found her.

Tarragon too had found a place to hide.

"That silver dome looks like a good place to hide," he said to himself.

He was walking towards the strawberry gateau which Zelda had so carefully covered before she went to bed. There was just enough room to squeeze underneath one of the crinkled up parts of the foil. It looked a little like the entrance to a shining cave. Just the sort of place to appeal to a fairy like Tarragon.

"I'll be able to show the others this lovely place when I've been found" thought Tarragon.

"It smells delicious too!"

He edged his way into what he thought to be a tunnel - it was, in fact, the narrow space between the tin foil cover and the side of the gateau, which was covered in whipped cream with chopped nuts pressed into it all the way around the side of the round cake.

"I won't go too far in, or it won't be a fair place to hide" Tarragon really wanted to be found very much, and couldn't wait to show the others and explore this wonderful place more with them.

"...96, 97, 98, 99, 100!" finished Tabasco.

"Coming! Ready or not!" he shouted.

Both fairies heard the call from their hiding places and waited excitedly to be found.

Tabasco looked behind the biscuit tin, behind the coffee jar, in Zelda's cups and bowls on the shelves..... but he couldn't find either of them.

"Now, I bet Coriander will be somewhere clean and lovely."

He tried the washing up bowl, then as he looked up he spotted the fruit basket on the window sill.

Up he climbed, and saw the silver glint of Coriander's hair.

"Found you!" he called out and helped Coriander climb delicately out of her hiding place.

"Now come and help me find Tarragon" he said.

The two fairies started looking. They searched everywhere they could think of.; in the cupboards, behind tins and packets on the shelves, they even looked in their salad bowl, but no.

Tarragon had not gone back to bed! They knew it would soon be dawn, and Vanilla and Cinnamon would be calling for them to go back to their cupboard.

"Let's call him" said Coriander.

"Tarragon, Tarragon" called Tabasco crossly[22], he hated being beaten.

"Tell us where you are Tarragon, we give up" called Coriander.

Tarragon heard them and he was very relieved. He had long since lost interest in his new hiding place and the

---

[22] Grumply

smell was making him feel sick now. He also felt a bit wet, sticky and uncomfortable down one side of his body, where he had been leaning against the side of the gateau. He edged his way back the way he had come in and emerged from the entrance to his shiny cave, just as the other two, now joined by an anxious looking Vanilla and Cinnamon, were walking up to the dome and looking in wonder at the new shiny object.

What they saw when they looked made them stop and stare. Tarragon, no longer smart and spruced up, was covered all over in the cream and nut mixture. Squeezing out hurriedly from his hiding place, had completed the covering all over him. At first they did not recognize him, but then he spoke and they all burst out laughing.

"Trust you, Tarragon" said Vanilla,

"You just can't stay clean for five minutes!"

"Never mind" said a smiling Cinnamon,

"Cleaning him up this time will be a tasty treat!"

They fell asleep a bit later that morning with the delicious taste of the creamy mixture on their tongues, except for Tarragon, who really did not want any!

Vanilla had, of course, waited until they were all

asleep, then taking her precious and trusted wand she tiptoed across the worktop to where the gateau stood. She had guessed what had happened, and knew a touch of magic was needed to put things right.

That done, she too went happily to sleep.

The strawberry gateau was in the middle of the table, the centrepiece of the party spread. Zelda and the four children sat around the table listening as the director of "Cooking with Zelda" made a short speech.

"Well, another series of this splendid show has come to an end!" he said smiling.

"It has been an especially good season, and for that we have to thank not just Zelda, but also her four young helpers. Now would you all come up here so that I can present you with your golden *Zelda* medals"

Oscar, Sarah, Hayley and Izzy walked proudly up, and the director placed the medals hung on smart orange cord around each of their necks in turn. Everyone clapped them and Zelda cheered.

Sitting back down at the table, the director asked Zelda to cut the gateau. When everyone had a nice big slice on their plates he took a big bite.

"This is delicious, a magical taste!" he declared with his mouth still full of cake.

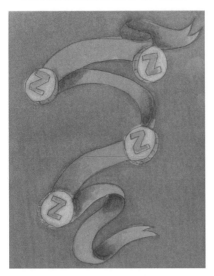

"Perhaps, you have fairies living in your kitchen making magic!" said Oscar.

"Oh yes, with silver wings!" said Hayley excitedly.

"And sparkly powder blue dresses!" exclaimed Sarah wide eyed.

"And glittery wands." added Izzy.

The girls all looked dreamy thinking of the beautiful clothes the fairies might wear.

"There would be boy fairies, too" said Oscar.

"And they would not be wearing dresses!"

Everyone laughed.

"Now that would be amazing to have fairies living in my kitchen" said Zelda

"I really wish it were true!"

ABOUT THE AUTHOR

Originating from Birkenhead, near Liverpool, **Cate Zorn** has lived in Asia for twelve years and in Spain for seventeen years. During her career as Primary school teacher and head teacher, she has always written tales for pleasure, lately especially for her four grandchildren. She now lives in Perth, Western Australia, since 2020, where she met and married her husband, and has two daughters. Zorn has an active social lifestyle: she does voluntary work by mentoring teenagers and works with adults with learning difficulties. She practises Pilates and aromatherapy.